HAUNTED HOSPITAL

Marty Chan

orca currents

ORCA BOOK PUBLISHERS

Published in Canada and the United States in 2020 by Orca Book Publishers.
orcabook.com

Library and Archives Canada Cataloguing in Publication
Title: Haunted hospital / Marty Chan.
Names: Chan, Marty, author.
Series: Orca currents.
Description: Series statement: Orca currents
Identifiers: Canadiana (print) 20200178768 | Canadiana (ebook) 20200178776 |
ISBN 9781459826205 (softcover) | ISBN 9781459826212 (PDF) |
ISBN 9781459826229 (EPUB)
Classification: LCC PS8555.H39244 H38 2020 | DDC jc813/.54—dc23

Library of Congress Control Number: 2020930587

Summary: In this high-interest accessible novel for middle readers,
four young teens find themselves in serious danger during a
role-playing game in a supposedly abandoned hospital.

Orca Book Publishers is committed to reducing the consumption of
nonrenewable resources in the making of our books. We make
every effort to use materials that support a sustainable future.

Orca Book Publishers gratefully acknowledges the support for its publishing
programs provided by the following agencies: the Government of Canada,
the Canada Council for the Arts and the Province of British Columbia
through the BC Arts Council and the Book Publishing Tax Credit.

Edited by Tanya Trafford
Design by Ella Collier
Cover image by Gettyimages.ca/zodebala
Author photo by Ryan Parker

Printed and bound in Canada.

23 22 21 20 • 1 2 3 4

WITHDRAWN

ED
HOSPITAL

In honor of Frank Nigro.

Thank you for inspiring me

to chase my dreams.

Chapter One

The light from Li's phone shone a path in the dark cemetery. She crept between the tombstones, trying to still her shaking hand.

Crack!

She spun around. The leafless trees behind her looked like skeletal fingers reaching for the bright moon.

"Who's there?" Li asked.

No answer.

She zipped up her fleece jacket, bracing herself against the brisk wind. She looked at the text on her phone again.

Find Tamara Reyes

Her mission was to find the gravestone marked with the name Tamara Reyes. It was part of the game *Spirits and Specters*. Li and her friends were the ghost hunters. Li had been given a solo assignment. She had to find evidence of the supernatural to earn bonus points.

She aimed her phone light at a nearby gravestone. Not the one she needed. She pointed the flashlight beam at a second one. Nope. Another tombstone and another. She crept along the line of markers, scanning each inscription.

Crack!

Li froze. It sounded like something or someone stepping on a dead branch. Was she being followed? She held her breath for a moment and listened. Nothing but the wind whistling through the trees.

"Get a hold of yourself, girl," she muttered. "It's a game. Just a game."

She picked up the pace. Soon her quick walk had turned into a fast jog. But even at her new pace, the light of her phone caught the tombstone she was looking for.

Here lies Tamara Reyes

1923–1971

Li grinned. "Found you," she said.

She inched toward the marker. The beam of light from her phone caught a dark shape on the grass. It was a wooden box about the size of a shoebox. Strange etchings snaked across the rosewood top. They looked like demon figures writhing in pain.

She texted a message to the game's referee.

Crypt Keeper, I found a box. Now what?

Three dots appeared on the screen. Li tapped her foot, waiting for the reply. She wanted to get out of the dead zone as fast as possible. *Ping.*

Open it.

Li stared at the box. Something about it made her nervous. Why couldn't she just bring the thing back so her teammates could open it with her? Safety in numbers and all that. But Li remembered that this was a solo mission. And she wasn't about to quit.

She carefully cracked the wooden lid open.

A bony hand shot out of the box. Li screamed and dropped her phone. She scrambled backward, slamming her elbow against a tombstone.

The skeleton hand bounced up and down on a metal spring like a creepy jack-in-the-box.

Li focused on slowing down her breathing. When she was calm, she started sweeping her hands over the grass until she could feel her phone.

Nice one, Priya. What now?

A few seconds later, the response pinged on the screen.

Ha! Did it freak you? Look inside.

Li crawled across the grass to grab the box. A folded-up piece of paper was jammed into one corner. Li plucked it out, opened the yellowed paper and read the scribbled words.

I cannot rest until I am reunited with my beloved.

She flipped the note over, but the other side was blank. She shone the light on Tamara Reyes's gravestone, noting the inscription at the bottom:

Loving wife to Denton Reyes.

Li skimmed the names on the nearby markers. None belonged to Denton Reyes. She headed to the next row.

Crack!

She scanned the cemetery for the source of the sound. Nothing. Li grabbed the box and scurried away, keeping low and out of sight. She wasn't about to stay in this spooky place a moment longer. The wind blew against her body, almost as if trying to prevent her escape.

Li's friends, Xander, Omar and Priya, all stood at the gate entrance, clapping.

"We have...to find out...where...Denton Reyes is buried," Li said, barely able to catch her breath.

Xander clapped Li on the back. Omar lowered the scarf wrapped around his face and took the wooden box from her. Priya strode over to a nearby tombstone and checked the binder sitting on top.

"Not bad, Li. Not bad at all," Priya said. "I'm awarding you fifty experience points for that mission."

"Fifty? Come on, Crypt Keeper," Li said. "That was worth at least a hundred points. The bony hand! That's got to be worth something."

Omar asked, "What hand?"

"Open the box," Li said.

"Okay. I don't see what—yikes!" The skeletal hand shot out at Omar's chest. He leapt back, dropping the box.

Xander laughed. "Chicken."

Li chuckled. "Never saw anyone jump that high."

"I wasn't scared," Omar said, eyeing the skeletal hand nervously.

"Yeah right." Li turned to the Crypt Keeper. "C'mon, Priya, why didn't I get more points? I finished the mission."

Priya shook her head. "Li, the game's called *Spirits and Specters*. Not Bicker and Complain. And actually you did not complete your mission. If you had found Denton Reyes's grave, you would have picked up the extra fifty points, but you didn't complete the task."

"Not my fault," Li argued. "There was no grave marker nearby. Plus, it sounded like someone else was in the cemetery."

"Oooo," Xander moaned. "You've angered the ghost of Tamara Reyes."

Omar joined in. "She wants to feed on your eyes."

Li sneered at them. "Act your age. Not your shoe size."

Towering over Xander and Li, Omar cocked his head. "But my age *is* the same as my shoe size."

Xander lifted up ghost arms and floated around Li. "Oooo."

"Cut it out, Xander," Li said, her nostrils flaring. Her nose stud sparkled in the moonlight. "So, Priya, where is Denton Reyes?"

The Crypt Keeper shook her head. "That's up to the next ghost hunter to find."

Omar shot his hand up. "My turn. I'll do it."

"Careful," Li said. "I really did think I heard someone. Might be security."

"So what?" Omar said. "We're not doing anything wrong. Come on, Priya. Give me my mission."

Xander leaned against the iron gate. "We do this every time! I'll bet Priya's big brother is lurking around, waiting to jump out at us. Same ol' same ol'."

Priya clutched her binder against her jacket. "You don't like my campaign missions?"

Xander said, "No, they're great. All I'm saying is that part of the fun of ghost hunting is visiting new and abandoned places. Right, Omar?"

Omar kicked at the ground with his high-top and glanced up sheepishly at Priya. "If there was a chance to hunt ghosts in another place...well... I guess...I wouldn't complain."

Priya turned to Li. "Do you feel the same way, Li?"

Li took a second to answer. "Well, I do love the jump scares."

"Me too! But the setting is a little...you know... played out," Omar said.

Xander sighed. "I wish we could find a new place."

Priya lowered her binder. "Yeah, I guess the graveyard is getting a bit tired. Tell you what. Next week we'll start looking around for another place. Whoever finds the best location gets to be the next Crypt Keeper."

They all nodded in agreement.

"Sounds like a plan," said Xander.

Chapter Two

The following week Xander peppered his friends with his ideas for new places to play. They ranged from the old Edmonton Oilers hockey arena to the river valley to an abandoned house a few blocks from the school.

None of his pitches landed with Omar or Li. Priya liked the abandoned-house idea until Li pointed out that the place was probably full of rats, cockroaches and dirty needles.

In language arts class, Xander tapped Omar's shoulder.

"I've got it. What about our school?" he whispered. "Built in the 1800s. Old. Creaky floors. They say a teacher died of the Spanish flu at the end of the First World War and now her ghost walks the hallways. Doors slam and buzzers go off at weird hours. I heard teachers don't want to work here at night."

Omar leaned back in his seat and whispered, "I spend enough time at this place. Don't make me come back more than I have to."

"Well, at least think about it," Xander said. "I heard the basement is super gross."

"Yeah? So is the bathroom after my dad is done using it, but that doesn't mean I want to check it out."

After school Xander kept hounding his friends. "I'm telling you, the school is the perfect setting. Just look at the place. Twisted, right?"

Priya stared at the three-story building. Ivy covered much of the red brick walls. "It's not a terrible idea, Xander."

"Hating it," Omar said. "It would feel like detention."

"What if we got caught?" Li asked. "Dad already thinks I spend too much time playing *Spirits and Specters*. He'd hit the roof if I was breaking and entering to stay in the game."

"Fine, fine," Xander grumbled. "I'll keep thinking."

"You know what?" Priya said. "We might be able to do something around the old train tunnel by the university. I bet it looks pretty sick at night."

Xander smiled. "I like that idea."

Li shook her head. "They're building condos on the site."

"You sure?" Priya asked.

"Yes," Li said. "My mom is selling the condo units. The whole area is chained off, and there's a security guard on duty 24/7. There's no way we'd get in there."

"Too bad," Omar said. "I like trains."

They kept walking. Xander zipped up his jacket to protect himself from the wind, but the zipper snagged.

"The old museum," Priya said. "What about there?"

Omar beamed. "Yeah! Now that all the collections have been moved to the new museum, I bet the old one is totally empty."

"And there are plenty of cool places on the old grounds to run around in," Li said.

Xander finally unjammed his zipper but accidentally smacked his chin with his hand and nearly knocked his glasses off. As he adjusted the frames on his face, he spotted a fenced-off building down a side street. Curious, he walked a few steps down the block to get a better look. A smile crept across his face. He raced back to his friends.

"Come check this out!" he said. "I may have found our spot."

"Better than the museum?" Omar scoffed. "Doubt it."

"Where?" Li asked.

Xander led the group to the building. Standing eight stories tall, the structure behind the blue chain-link fence towered over the teens. The main-floor windows and entrances were covered with sheets of plywood. Taggers had spray-painted the lower-level walls. Some of the second- and third-floor windows were broken.

"George Wickerman Hospital," Xander announced. "The haunted hospital."

Li shivered. "Oh man, I totally forgot about this place. Twisted."

"Why would they shut down a hospital?" Omar asked.

Xander looked at Omar. "Right, I forgot that this went down before you came to our school. The hospital's been closed forever."

Li chimed in. "More like five years."

"Sure, sure," Xander said. "They say it was originally a place for really sick patients. People who came down with TB—tuberculosis. And that in the

1950s the government started to run secret tests on the patients."

"Why?" Omar asked.

"Because it didn't matter if they lived or died. There was no cure for them, so the doctors were free to do experiments to see how different chemicals would affect their bodies."

"I heard it wasn't TB patients," Li said. "I heard it was orphans."

"Can you let me tell the story?" Xander said.

"Sorry."

"Anyway," Xander continued, "they shut down the hospital when a bunch of bodies were found. The patients who didn't survive the tests were tossed into a dumpster. After that normal people started to come down with a mystery disease. The doctors. Then the nurses. Then patients who went in for broken arms or something. It spread fast, killing several people. No one knew the cause or the cure, so the government shut down the hospital, like, twenty years ago."

"Five," said Li.

"Stop fact-checking me, Li."

Li shrugged. "Facts are important."

Omar peered through the fence. "Nasty."

"Here's the twisted thing," Xander said. "They say the ghosts of the dead walk the halls even to this day."

Li joined Omar at the fence. "I remember hearing stories about this place when I was in elementary school. I can't believe we didn't think of it before."

"We never walk down this way," Xander said. "But it's totally got what we're looking for. Exciting new territory, a little danger..."

Priya peered at the building. "I don't know."

"I heard that this guy, Josh—you remember him?" said Xander. "A couple of years ahead of us? Yeah, well, I heard he went to check it out last year. No one has seen him since."

"I heard his dad got a job in Saskatoon," Li said.

"He vanished," Xander said, glaring at his friend. "Without a trace."

Omar pushed back from the fence. "I love the place. If it looks this creepy on the outside, I can only imagine what it looks like on the inside."

"After five years it would be pretty run-down," Li said.

Priya squinted at the building. "How would we even get in?"

"I'm sure they would have security," Li said.

"You always think that," Omar said. "If they did have security, how would the taggers have marked up the walls?"

"The windows on the main floor are boarded up," Priya noted. "And no way are we going to reach the second-floor windows."

"Too bad we can't get inside," Xander said. "That would be the ultimate."

"Well, I guess it wasn't meant to be," said Priya. "But I can check out the old museum over the weekend. Even if we can't get inside there, we should be able to at least explore the grounds."

The four of them turned and started to head for their regular route home.

After a few paces Xander stopped. "You all go ahead," he said. "I'll see you tomorrow."

When the other three had gone around the corner, Xander turned back and circled the haunted hospital, searching for some way in. From the street the place looked locked up tight, but what about up close?

He glanced around for any witnesses. An old man was raking leaves in his yard, but his back was to Xander. The coast was clear. Xander climbed the fence and scurried to one of the boarded-up windows. He pushed against the plywood. Solid. He crept farther along the wall, testing each boarded-up window for a way in. No luck. Then he reached a section of the building hidden from the street by a row of bushes. As he neared the window, he began to smile at what he had discovered.

The sheet of plywood was loose.

Chapter Three

Xander had found a way in. He pried the plywood sheet farther away from the window and crawled inside. His jacket snagged on a loose nail and tore a hole in the shoulder. Xander stuck a finger through the hole in the fabric and shook his head.

"Mom is totally going to kill me," he muttered.

He fished his phone out of his back pocket and switched on the flashlight mode. He swept the beam across the walls of the dusty room. The place reeked.

Xander headed to the door and pulled it open. The hinges groaned as the door swung inward. He poked his head into the hallway and flashed the light both ways. At one end was a large counter at the nurses' station. Beside the black-topped desk a gurney sat on its side, rusted caster wheels dangling from the legs.

At the other end of the hallway, double doors led deeper into the heart of the haunted hospital. The scene reminded Xander of an old video game his dad used to play. *Silent Hill*. He remembered once sneaking a peek as his dad killed zombie nurses and having nightmares for a month.

A clang echoed from somewhere deep in the bowels of the building.

"What was that?" Xander asked. "Get a grip. It's nothing."

Talking aloud to himself helped calm his nerves. He took a breath and entered the hallway. The nurses' station would make a perfect home base for the game, he noted, and took a photo. He flipped the gurney back onto its wheels and pushed it against the counter. The metal frame squeaked and groaned, but it could still roll.

Suddenly a dark shape shot out from behind the station and scooted down the hallway. Xander aimed the light at it, his entire body throbbing with instant adrenaline.

"What was that?"

He crept toward the double doors.

"Who's here?" he asked, his voice barely above a whisper. "Anyone here—"

Hiss-ss-ss!

Xander froze as a gray cat bolted past him and zipped behind the nurses' station. Xander clutched the phone against his chest. He could feel his heart pounding.

"Okay, kitty. Nice kitty. Stupid kitty."

Once his heart rate had returned to normal, Xander began to explore the maze of hallways that twisted and turned deeper and deeper into the building. He checked each of the rooms along the way. Some were empty. A couple still had beds in them. He took photos of potential sites that might work for *Spirits and Specters*.

And it was giving him some story ideas. He tapped the voice-recorder app on his phone and spoke into it.

"Alison Rigby died in this very room on a chilly winter night," he said, recounting some of the details from the legend he had researched. They would be great for the mission setup. "Even though she had contracted TB, she might have lived longer if the doctors hadn't injected her with experimental drugs. Her screams filled the hallways. The medical staff observed the poor woman gasping for air in her final moments. She died in utter pain and fear. Now her spirit walks the halls." When he was done, he played it back. "Not bad, if I do say so myself. I just need more haunted rooms for inspiration."

He propped the door open with a rubber doorstop he had found on the floor and noted the room number—176. He navigated new corridors, identifying landmarks to help him find his way back. His light flashed on an Exit sign. The door opened to a stairwell. But Xander couldn't go up or down. A giant tangle of barbed wire was nailed across both flights of stairs.

Xander spoke into his phone. "Stick to the main floor. No sense in wrecking more of my clothes."

He headed out of the stairwell and explored the rest of the corridor. Another set of double doors loomed in the distance. He aimed his light at them.

Two eyes reflected back at him from behind one of the windows. "What the heck?" When Xander looked closer, the eyes were gone.

"Stupid cat," he muttered. "Had to be the cat. Right? Yeah. And why are you still talking to yourself, man? Get a grip."

Xander's feet suddenly felt like he had stepped in wet concrete. He raised the phone and aimed the beam of light at the closed doors again. No sign of the eyes.

"Must have been my imagination." He turned on the recorder app. "If I can figure out how to make something that looks like reflecting eyes, Li will lose her mind. Note to self—buy marbles and string."

Xander willed his feet to move forward. He inched closer to the doors, keeping the light trained on the windows. His legs tingled with anticipation.

He carefully pushed one of the doors open. A rush of air and dust swirled up. He shone the light down the hallway.

"Whoa. The gang is going to love this place."

Xander thought for a second about whether he should continue to explore. He swept the flashlight beam along the walls and doors. Two gurneys were off to one side, some large cardboard boxes on the other. The hallway looked pretty much like the others. He decided he had seen enough and turned away.

As he made his way back through the maze of corridors, he switched his camera to video mode and filmed everything. A video map of the hospital layout would be useful for planning their stories.

He neared a corridor blocked off with a web of yellow hazard tape, and the stench of mold and mildew shot up his nose. He shone his light through the web. Parts of the ceiling had fallen down, and water dripped onto the floor. The floor was shiny with some kind of gross green gunk.

He spoke into his phone. "Watch out for places with yellow warning tape. Parts of the building aren't really safe. Try to score some hospital gowns and bedsheets for set decoration and wardrobe. Maybe at the thrift store? Ooh, yeah. If we can find some surgical masks, definitely get those."

He stepped away from the yellow tape.

"Working my way back to home base," he said. "Rooms 176, 148, 112 and 129 are all great. Need some chalk to mark off the halls so people don't get lost."

He continued to film until he reached the nurses' station. Then he checked the video. Although the images were dark, they provided enough sense of the layout to help him plan out the missions.

Xander's chest tightened. Did he just see what he thought he saw? He rewound the clip. They only appeared for a second, but yes, he was almost certain he had captured a second set of eyes in a window as he filmed his return to the nurses' station. But it must have been a trick of the light. Maybe all this talk of ghosts was making Xander see things. He didn't really believe all the stories he told. He just loved getting his friends worked up.

Xander looked around, unable to shake the feeling that he was being watched.

"If there are ghosts here," he shouted, "show yourselves!"

The cat growled from behind the counter.

"You got some friends back there, little kitty?" Xander asked.

The cat hissed.

"No? Okay, I'll leave you in peace. Next time, if you're nicer to me, I'll bring you some treats."

Xander headed out. He glanced down the corridor one last time. "This mission is going to be so great."

Chapter Four

The next day Xander waited outside the school for his friends. He couldn't wait to fill them in. Omar and Li arrived first. Right behind them was Priya, an overstuffed backpack slung over one shoulder. She leaned so far forward she looked like an old woman walking against the wind.

"You aren't going to believe what I found!" Xander said.

Omar's face lit up. "The winning lottery ticket for the fifty-million-dollar jackpot? The answers for next week's math test? My missing Nintendo Switch?"

"No. I found a way in!" Xander said.

"To what?" Priya asked.

"The haunted hospital."

Li gasped. "No way. How?"

Xander explained how he had discovered the loose sheet of plywood over the window and described the creepy hallways he had explored. Omar and Li hung on every word. Priya stared at her feet.

"So would it be okay if we cut Priya's mission short and started a new one in the hospital?" asked Xander.

"I am in," said Omar and started doing a little dance.

Li laughed. "You are such a goof. Okay, Xander. I'm in too."

"What do you say, Priya?" asked Xander.

Priya frowned. "I don't know. I still haven't checked out the museum. Might be even creepier than the hospital."

"Come on," Xander pleaded. "The hospital is perfect. We don't have to worry about bad weather. And it is as twisted as anything I've ever seen."

Omar clasped his hands together. "Please, Priya."

Priya frowned. "But we haven't even given the museum a chance. Let me scout it out before we make any final decisions."

Li looked at her friend. "Maybe we can use the museum for our next mission. But this location sounds exciting. And we all agreed that the cemetery was getting boring. I say we put this to a vote."

Xander and Omar nodded.

"Well, it's obvious how that's going to go." Priya crossed her arms.

"Who's in favor of the hospital for our new mission site?" asked Li.

Everyone but Priya raised their hands.

Xander beamed. "Okay, it's settled. I'll be the next Crypt Keeper. Saturday night, we meet at the front of the hospital."

Priya didn't say another word.

On Saturday afternoon Xander returned to the hospital with his gear to set up for the mission. He double-checked to make sure no one was watching before he climbed over the metal fence.

He jogged across the parking lot and found the window with the loose plywood. He pried the wood open enough to toss his backpack into the room, then climbed inside. He strapped a headlamp around his head and snapped it on. The room reeked of mildew and cat urine.

Xander pulled a bag from his backpack and shook it.

"Hey, kitty, I got you some tuna nibbles. Want some?"

Xander's plan was to corner the cat and put it into some room away from the action. He knew Li was allergic to cats, and Omar would end up spending the entire game trying to befriend it.

"Here, kitty, kitty," Xander said as he shook the bag again.

The cat didn't come. After a few minutes Xander gave up. He pocketed the treats, grabbed his backpack and headed to the nurses' station. He stopped and stared at the overturned gurney beside the counter. Hadn't he set it on its wheels last time? His nerves were getting the better of him. He probably knocked the gurney over when the cat scared him. Or maybe it was defective.

He unloaded his backpack on the counter and sorted through the props. He laid out a couple of hospital gowns he had picked up from the thrift store, a box of chalk, surgical masks, a few plastic trays and a portable speaker. He also pulled out a makeshift map of the hospital layout that he had drawn up from his video footage. His plan was to start at the far end of the hospital and work his way back.

He scooped up the speaker and chalk, then headed around the corner. A desk and some chairs blocked the hallway doors. He cocked his head to one side, puzzled.

"Was this stuff here before?" he whispered.

He looked around, wondering if he had walked in the wrong direction.

"Weird," he said after a moment. "Must be my imagination."

He shoved the furniture out of the way and approached the first of the rooms he had staked out earlier. Room 176. The door he was sure he had propped open before was closed. He cracked it open, and something shot out between his legs. Xander shrieked and nearly dropped his speaker.

"Stupid cat," he muttered.

The mangy feline scampered to the nurses' station and hid behind the counter. Xander pulled the bag of treats from his pocket again. He shook a few out onto his palm, then tossed them on the floor.

"You hungry, little guy? Come and get it." He created a trail of treats on the floor, leading into one of the empty rooms.

After what seemed like forever, the cat came out and sniffed the treats. Xander inched back and watched as it scarfed one treat and sniffed the next. Slowly the cat followed the trail of treats. Xander got ready. When the cat was a few feet into the room, Xander closed the door, trapping the cat inside.

The cat yowled through the door.

"It's okay, kitty. I'll let you out when the game's done. Then you can have the rest of the treats."

He headed back to room 176. He turned on the speaker and placed it under the bed so that he could broadcast creepy sounds from it. Then he left a message in chalk on the wall—*You're Next*. As he wrote, he couldn't shake the feeling that someone was watching him. He ignored the impulse to look behind him.

Suddenly a female voice boomed from the speaker. "Your speaker is now connected."

Xander dropped the chalk and spun around. It took him a few minutes to calm down as he glared at the portable device. He'd forgotten about the auto notification. "Get a grip, Xander," he said as he picked up the chalk.

He went back to sketching. He glanced over his shoulder a few times to make sure he was alone.

Chapter Five

That evening Xander's friends gathered in the haunted hospital. Xander's headlamp illuminated his hand-drawn layout of the place, which he'd spread out on the counter. Priya adjusted the light strapped to her head. Li and Omar directed the glow from their phones onto the map as well.

"Awesome!" Omar said. "I've got goose bumps."

Li beamed at the new site for their game. "It's perfect," she said, sounding a bit stuffed up.

"I could do without the smell of cat piss," Priya snapped. "And the building looks like it's about to fall down." She was still unhappy about being overruled.

Xander ignored her comments. "George Wickerman Hospital was used in the 1950s to experiment on patients who were going to die anyway. A doctor working with a secret government agency injected a chemical compound called Digi-Tox into the patients to see what it would do. The government wanted to use this chemical to cure TB, but it did more harm than good. Within hours of the injection, the test subjects went into shock and started throwing up. Their eyes bled, and they experienced so much pain, all they could do was scream. They died within a day."

"Brutal," Omar said. "Remind me never to go to a hospital when I'm sick."

Li shushed him. "Not all hospitals are bad."

Priya didn't comment.

"This one is," Xander said. "And one of the patients who died was a woman named Alison Rigby. She had a promising career as a concert pianist."

Omar chuckled. "Heh, heh."

"Pi-an-ist," Xander said. "Anyway, Alison dreamed of playing in all the great concert halls around the world, but her dream ended tragically right here at the George Wickerman Hospital. In room 176."

Li peered over her shoulder at the dark corridor. "What happened after she died?"

"They say you can hear screams from the room at the exact moment she died—9:07 p.m."

Li checked her phone. "Seventeen minutes from now."

Omar shot his hand up. "I'm first. Let me go."

Xander pointed at his makeshift map. "Okay, Omar. Your mission is to get to room 176 and record any sounds. You have to stay there for at least fifteen minutes."

"No problem," Omar said.

"But be careful," Xander warned. "Avoid any areas that are blocked off with yellow tape."

"Why?"

"Because they're unsafe," Xander said. "For real."

Li leaned into Omar. "Mom said this place got major water damage from some heavy rains a few summers ago. That's why no developer wants to renovate it. Don't get yourself killed."

Omar took her hand. "If I don't make it back, my *Star Wars* collectibles are yours."

Priya sighed and rolled her eyes.

"Something wrong, Priya?" Xander asked.

"No. It's your mission. Run it the way you want," she replied.

"Maybe you would like to go on the mission first?" he asked. He assumed Priya was still mad about not being Crypt Keeper.

"No, I'm good," Priya mumbled.

"Okay," Omar said, holding up his phone.

"The recorder is ready. Wish me luck."

"Good luck," Li said, wiping her nose with her sleeve. Even with the cat tucked away, her allergies were acting up.

"You're going to need it," Xander said with a grin. "Text me when you're in the room."

"This is so awesome," Li said and then sneezed. "Even with the cat dander, this place is the creepiest."

Priya tried to smile.

Omar crept down the hall, his phone casting light across the dusty walls. He turned the corner and was gone. Xander rested his phone against his backpack and waited for the first text.

The moments ticked by. Li paced back and forth. Priya slouched against the counter. There wasn't a lot for them to do as they waited for Omar to finish his mission.

"How long has it been?" Li asked.

Xander swiped his phone screen awake. "Three minutes."

Time had turned into a slug, barely inching forward and sometimes remaining completely still. Xander glanced at his phone for the umpteenth time. It was now 9:05. Omar should have texted by now. What was taking him so long? Xander resisted the urge to call his friend. Part of the fun of the game was the tension of being alone and out of contact.

Li fidgeted from foot to foot. "Has he texted yet?"

Xander shook his head. "You know he hasn't. My phone's right there."

"Omar probably can't see the room numbers," Priya said. "At least the gravestones were clearly marked."

Xander bit his lower lip to keep from snapping at Priya. He swiped the phone screen again. Still no text.

A low moan echoed from down the hall.

Li stiffened. "What was that?"

They all fell silent and listened hard. Li pointed her light down the dusty corridor behind them. No sign of anyone.

Priya yawned. "Nice try, Xander. Using a portable speaker to bounce sound around the place. Bit of a cliché, but not bad."

"I'm not using a speaker here," Xander said.

"I used the same trick in the cemetery," said Priya.

Li's eyes widened. "All those cracks I heard were from you? That was so freaky!"

Priya held up her phone. "Sorry. They were just some sound effects I found online. I think the one we're hearing now is something called 'ghostly moans.' Am I right, Xander?"

"I swear it's not me," Xander said. "I mean, yes, I was using the speaker, but it's set up in room 176, not here. Maybe it's another stray cat."

"It doesn't sound like any cat I've ever heard," Li said. "Are you sure this isn't part of the game?"

"I'm not making this sound. Honest."

Priya crossed her arms. "Drop the innocent act. You're trying to freak Li out."

Another moan.

Li scurried over to stand beside Priya. "Maybe we should go," she said.

"No," Xander said. "The mission is just starting. It's an old hospital. The walls or the ceiling are shifting."

Priya pushed Li away. "Ow! Your fingernails are digging into my skin."

Xander peered down the passage. No sign of anything alive. Or dead.

"Text Omar," Li said. "See if he's okay."

"Good idea," Priya said. "Ask him if he can hear anything."

Xander grabbed his phone. It was 9:07.

Where are you?

There was no reply. Not even the three dots on the screen to indicate that someone was typing. Xander waited for a few more minutes, his leg twitching. He thought he was the one who was supposed to do the scaring. Not the other way around.

"Well?" Li asked.

"He's not replying," Xander said. "Let me try again."

He typed another message.

Dude. You okay?

No response.

"Maybe the cell reception in here is bad," Priya suggested.

Li checked her phone and shook her head. "I have full bars. Let me try calling him." She tapped her screen and placed the phone to her ear. They waited.

"He should have answered by now," she said, lowering the phone. "Where could he be?"

Xander tried not to assume the worst. But one thing was certain. Omar was missing.

Chapter Six

Li drummed her fingers on the top of the rusty gurney. "Why isn't he answering his phone?"

Priya placed her hand on top of Li's to stop her nervous drumming. "Relax, Li. There could be a number of reasons he's not answering. We might have cell coverage here, but the wing he's in might be shielded."

"I'm sure he's okay," Xander said. Then he shouted down the hallway, "How's it going, Omar?"

No answer.

Li said, "What if he's trapped or hurt? Remember what my mom said about all the water damage? A piece of the ceiling might have fallen on him or something."

"The areas I marked off for the game looked pretty safe," Xander said and then stopped. "Unless he went down one of the halls that was taped off."

Li and Priya looked at each other. They were all starting to freak.

"Phone him again," Priya said to Li. "Maybe we'll hear his ringtone."

Li did. They strained to listen for the familiar *da-DA, dun-dun-dun DA da*.

They thought they heard something behind them. Xander shuddered. Li clutched her phone.

"Game's over," Priya said. "We have to find Omar."

"Yes," Li said. "We can't wait for him any longer."

"We never should have come here," Priya added.

Xander glared at her. He wanted to remind her that they had all agreed. Instead he said, "I'm sure he's going to be all right."

"Where did you send him?" Li asked.

"Room 176. Down that way."

"Let's go." Li sprinted down the hall, switching on her phone light to illuminate the way. "Omar! We're coming," she called out.

Xander shot a look at Priya. "Well?"

"After you, Crypt Keeper," she said.

They rounded the corner, and Xander caught up to Li. "The room's down this way."

His headlamp felt warm against his forehead, but not as hot as his cheeks, which burned with frustration. How had the mission gone off the rails so quickly?

The light bounced off the walls, revealing something he hadn't noticed earlier. Several red slashes marked one of the doors. He slowed for a second, concentrating his beam of light on the strange markings.

Li gasped. "Is that *blood*?"

"No, it's all part of my mission setup," Xander lied. He didn't want the others to know he wasn't in full command.

"You sure that's not Omar's blood?"

"Yes, I'm sure," he said, swinging his headlamp away from the marked door. "The room's down this way."

He crept ahead.

A definitely moan-like sound came from behind them. Xander spun around. No one was there. Li instinctively crouched into a defensive fighting position.

Priya patted her shoulder. "It's okay. Relax."

Another low moan.

"Spooky moans we can't identify are NOT okay!" shouted Li, her fists clenched. "It's the ghosts! I know it! What do you want from us?" she asked, turning around and addressing the empty hallway.

No answer.

Priya shot Xander a look. "Are you messing with us?"

"This is not my doing," he said. "I swear."

"Omar's probably pulling a prank on us," Priya told Li. "I'll bet Xander put him up to it."

Another moan from the darkness.

"That doesn't sound like Omar," Li said. "Besides, how could he get behind us?"

"This place is a maze," Priya said. "He could have found a way to loop around. We're onto you, Omar!"

No answer. They waited for several moments, which felt like forever in the dark hallway. The moaning had stopped. For now.

Xander pointed ahead. "Room 176 is right over here."

They hustled toward the room. Xander's hand trembled as he pressed his palm against the door and pushed it open. He dreaded what or who might be inside.

The room was empty.

Li peered over Xander's shoulder and asked, "Where is he?"

Xander leaned back to check the room number on the wall beside the door. It was 176. He glanced inside again.

The bed was in the middle of the room. The chalk message was on the wall above the bed. He lowered himself to the floor and peeked under the frame. The portable speaker sat on the dusty floor just where he had left it.

He retrieved the black box, turned it off and stuffed it into his backpack.

"I knew you were messing with us," Priya said.

Xander shook his head. "This is the only one I planted."

A moan came from outside the room.

Priya shot him a look.

"I swear this is the only one," Xander said.

"Maybe you're getting Omar to use his phone to scare us," Priya said accusingly. "Phone him again,

Li. Quick. If he's nearby we'll hear the ringtone."

Li dialed her phone and waited. The first few bars of the *Star Wars* theme sounded down the hallway.

"Omar!" Li said.

"I knew it," Priya said.

She stepped out of the room and scanned the corridor. The theme song started over. Her headlamp swiveled from one door to another as she advanced toward the sound. Xander and Li were only a few steps behind her.

Priya got as close as she could to where the sound was coming from. She glanced around. On the floor, tucked behind an open door, was Omar's phone. She knelt down and picked it up. The caller ID showed Li calling.

Li grabbed the phone from Priya's hand. "He would *never* leave this behind. Not for anything."

"Maybe he's in one of the other rooms," said Xander. "We should split up and search them."

Priya's eyes widened. "Haven't you ever watched a horror movie? You *never* split up! We stay together."

"Okay, okay, but we need to check all the rooms."

"Then let's get started," said Li. "Omar! If you can hear me, say something!"

"*Leave this place,*" a ghostly voice moaned.

Xander froze. "You both heard that, didn't you?"

Priya nodded. Li shone her phone light down the hall. No sign of anyone.

"*Leave now,*" another ghostly voice moaned.

"They're all around us," Li said.

A chorus of voices. "*Leave this place.*"

"I think maybe we should listen to them," Priya said.

"We can't leave without Omar," Li said.

A rhythmic beating of metal on metal echoed in front of them. Xander backed up, keeping his light trained on the passage in front of him.

"Return to the home base," he ordered.

"What about Omar?" Li asked, refusing to budge.

Priya grabbed Li's hand and hauled her back. "If he's smart, he got out of here already."

The beating got closer. A shadowy figure emerged from one of the rooms down the hall. At first Xander hoped it might be Omar, but this figure was too short. Another figure emerged from a different room. And a third appeared from yet another room.

"Run!" Xander shouted. "Now!"

He pushed the girls ahead as he broke into a full-on sprint. The chorus of ghostly voices shouted behind the trio.

"Leave! Go! Never return!"

Xander sped around the corner. At the nurses' station, three gurneys had been stacked on top of each other to form a barricade.

"This way!" Xander screamed as he scrambled to the room with the window they had entered through.

"Xander, wait!" Priya called.

Xander couldn't hear anything other than the sound of his own panicked breathing. He crashed into the room, zipped toward the window and squeezed through the gap. Then he streaked across the lawn to the metal fence.

He looked back at the haunted hospital, resting his hands on his knees and sucking the crisp air into his burning lungs.

Priya finally caught up to him. "Didn't you hear me calling you?" she said.

He panted for air. "No. I...was...too busy trying to save us."

"Us?" Priya said, raising an eyebrow.

Xander straightened up. "Hey. Where's Li?"

"That's what I was trying to tell you," Priya said. "She ran off."

"Where?"

She pointed back at the dark hospital.

"You mean she's still inside?" he asked.

"Yes! She said she wasn't going to leave Omar behind." She looked down for a moment before continuing. "Xander. You know what we have to do. We have to go back."

Chapter Seven

Xander stared at his friend in disbelief. "Priya, why didn't you grab her?"

"You don't think I tried?" she shot back. "And what about you? You ran out of there so fast I'm surprised you didn't leave your sneakers behind."

Xander couldn't look Priya in the eye. "Well, never mind who did what. We have to figure out what to do now."

"I know exactly what we're going to do." She pulled a phone from her back pocket. "We're calling the police."

Xander grabbed her wrist. "Wait. Not so fast."

"Our friends are inside, Xander. Who knows what's happening to them right now?"

Xander pleaded with her. "Think this through for a second. What are you going to tell the cops? That ghosts are in the haunted hospital? They'll just laugh at us. And then they might charge us with trespassing."

"No they won't."

"Imagine you're a cop listening to this story," Xander said. " 'Officer, we were sneaking around the haunted hospital, and some ghosts grabbed our friends. Can you save them from the spirits?' After hearing that, would you want to help?"

She lowered her phone. "I guess not. What do you suggest we do?"

"To be honest, I don't have a clue."

She glanced at the building, then back at her phone.

"Even if we did call the cops, it would take them forever to get here. We need to figure out a way to—hey!" Xander called after Priya, who was racing toward the building.

"I'm going back in!" Priya shouted.

"Wait for me!"

Xander caught up to Priya at the window entrance. She climbed in. Xander followed, lighting the way with his headlamp. He wasn't crazy about being back inside. He sincerely hoped they found their friends before the ghosts found them.

Priya snapped on her lamp as they stepped into the hallway. The gurneys were still stacked beside the counter at the nurses' station. Xander remembered the stories he had read about poltergeists—bratty spirits that liked to move furniture around and knock on walls. He wondered if they had rearranged the gurneys. Could they also grab people?

"It looks like the ghosts don't want us to go this way," Xander said.

Priya veered toward the unblocked hall. "The last time I saw Li, she was running this way."

Priya jogged in the direction of room 176, but instead of turning the corner, she headed straight toward a set of double doors.

"I think she was going toward the children's unit," she said.

Xander raised an eyebrow. "How do you know where that is?"

Priya swung her headlamp at the sign on the wall. *Children's Unit*. A green arrow pointed in the same direction she was going.

"Good eye," said Xander.

Priya pushed the double doors open and crept toward the large counter at the crossroads of four intersecting hallways. She noticed traces of footsteps in the dust.

"Li must have gone this way," she said, pointing to the left.

She jogged down the corridor, Xander following close behind. He peeked over his shoulder for any sign of ghosts. There had been no moaning since he and Priya had sneaked back into the hospital. He started to wonder if they had imagined it all earlier.

"Looks like she headed for the cancer ward," Priya said.

Xander thought for moment. "How do you know this place so well, Priya?" he asked.

Ignoring his question, she whispered, "There's more than one set of footprints."

Xander peered down. She was right. Multiple footprints marked the tiled floor.

"Maybe Li got turned around and retraced her steps," Xander suggested. "Or Omar."

"Or someone else is here," Priya said. "And not a supernatural kind of someone."

"You're sure some of these footprints are Li's?"

Priya shrugged. "I can't be sure of anything right now, but this is our best lead."

They slid along the wall, following the trail of footprints. It was clear now that there were at least six different sets. She turned to Xander, her lamp light shining directly in his eyes.

"Do you think someone took her and Omar?"

Xander shrugged. "I don't—"

Suddenly something grabbed Priya's shoulder. Xander yelped. Priya spun around.

Li stepped out. She squinted against the glare of Priya's headlamp. "It's me," she whispered as she shielded her eyes.

Priya pulled Li close and hugged her. "We thought we'd lost you."

"I thought it was you," Xander said, acting like it was no big deal to see her there.

"Yeah, that's why you screamed like a five-year-old," said Li.

"I did not."

"Did too."

He changed the subject. "Why were you hiding in that room?"

Li motioned the two to step into the room with her. "It's safer in here. They shouldn't be able to find us."

"Who?" Xander asked.

"I followed them to this point, but I thought they might have heard me, so I slipped into this room to hide."

"Who?" Priya asked.

"Are they ghosts?" asked Xander.

Li shook her head. "They seemed real enough to me. I don't know who they are, but they're definitely not ghosts."

"Oh man, this is my fault," Xander said. "I should never have pushed for the haunted hospital. I'd settle for the boring old cemetery right about now."

Priya looked at him. "It wasn't *that* boring."

"Sorry," he said.

"But where is Omar?" Priya asked Li.

"I don't know. But I'm sure the people I followed have something to do with his disappearance."

Xander inched closer to his friends. "Where did they go?"

Li pointed down the hallway.

"We have to find them," Priya said.

"Turn off your lights," Li ordered. "We don't want them to see us coming."

Xander and Priya snapped off their headlamps. Li tapped her phone screen and covered the soft blue glow with her hand. Xander couldn't believe this was the same girl who had jumped at the slightest noise in the cemetery. She was calm and focused.

"You two ready?" she asked.

Priya nodded.

Xander choked out, "Yes."

"Then let's roll," Li said.

Chapter Eight

Li led Xander and Priya toward the end of the dark corridor. She hugged the wall until she reached an intersection. She peered around the corner. She motioned the others to follow. Her phone lit up chairs stacked in front of a set of double doors. On closer inspection Xander noticed a narrow gap through the blockade of chairs.

Li put a finger to her lips, signaling for silence, then slid between the chairs and pushed one of the doors open. Xander went next. He bumped into a chair, making it scrape across the floor. He froze.

"Shhh!" Li hissed.

"Sorry," he whispered. He squeezed his arms tight against his body and inched toward his friends.

On the other side of the doors, more furniture had been stacked in what looked like an obstacle course. Li climbed over a gurney and slid between two tall filing cabinets.

"Who would set up this blockade?" Priya asked as she scrambled behind Li.

Xander shrugged. "I guess someone wants to be left alone."

"But why?" she asked.

"I don't know," he said.

"Will you two shut your mouths?" Li whispered. "They're going to hear us."

Xander fell silent. He wouldn't tell Li this, but he was very impressed with her and wondered how she had found the courage to do all this when she had been so scared.

Priya and Xander made their way through the obstacle course and reached Li, who stared at a trail of footprints leading to an exit.

"I think they were protecting this door," Priya said.

Li nudged Xander forward with her elbow. "Open it."

"Me? Why not you?"

She held up her phone. "I'm lighting the way."

"Fine, fine." Xander gingerly pulled the door open. On the other side was a stairwell. But this one was different than the first one he had explored. Barbed wire was nailed across the staircase leading up, but someone had snipped the wire that was supposed to block the steps to the basement.

Priya looked over his shoulder. "That's the way to the morgue."

"Are you sure?" Xander asked.

"I think."

Li gritted her teeth. "I bet we'll find Omar down there."

Xander peeked down the stairs. A faint light was coming from the lower level of the hospital. Someone or something was definitely down there.

Li said, "Let's go."

"You first, Priya," Xander suggested. "You seem to know your way around this hospital."

Priya didn't reply, just stepped in front of them and prepared to descend. Li tapped her phone screen and shut off the light. The glow from below was enough for the teens to navigate the stairs.

Xander waved at his friends. "Hold up."

He returned to the hallway and unscrewed a leg from a wooden chair. He hefted it, testing its weight.

It was solid enough to do some damage. He handed it to Li.

She stared at the chair leg. "Do you think we're going to need weapons?" she asked.

Xander answered, "We have to be ready for anything."

He unscrewed two more chair legs, one for Priya and one for himself. Once armed, they made their way down the stairs. The light below seemed to flicker. As they reached the landing and turned the corner, Priya spotted the source. Set beside an open door was an old-fashioned lantern. The candle wick inside cast an eerie orange glow on the walls.

Priya reached the bottom of the stairwell and peered through the open doorway. More lanterns were spaced out along a corridor that ended at a set of metal doors.

The gang crept in.

Xander gripped his chair leg, ready for an attack.

Priya eyed the doors along the corridor. She signaled the others to stop and listen.

They could make out a faint murmur of voices.

Xander glanced at Priya. She frowned and said, "I hear them too."

Li twisted her hands around her chair leg. "If they hurt Omar..."

Xander took a step toward the doors and spotted the sign above them. *Morgue.* "You were right," he said.

Priya shrugged.

"Omar has to be inside," Li whispered. "And alive."

She pressed her hand against one of the doors, but Priya grabbed her wrist. She tapped her right ear. They leaned closer to hear the voices on the other side.

"Dude, all you had to do was split," a gruff-sounding man said.

"I'm sorry. I didn't know you were here," said a familiar voice.

Li turned to the others. "That's him. It's Omar."

Priya put a finger to her lips. "Shh. We need to know how many people are in there."

A woman interrupted. "Quest, what's your bag, man? The plan was to scare the kids away, not take hostages."

The one called Quest answered, "Rainbow, let me think. Just chill."

"Please. Let me go," Omar pleaded.

"Took us a long time to set up our home here, dude," Quest said. "And you think we're going to let you go and tell the fuzz? No way. Winter is almost here, man. I don't plan on waiting in line at the shelter for a lumpy bed."

"I won't tell anyone. I swear," Omar said.

"Don't flip out, dude," the woman said. "We need time to think."

Xander stepped back and whispered to Li and

Priya, "They're squatters, I think. Homeless people living here."

Li shook her head. "No. They're kidnappers."

"Whoever they are, we have to get Omar away from them," Priya said. "We have to call the police."

Xander chewed his bottom lip, unsure. Li slid the chair leg under her arm and reached into a pocket to pull out her phone. As she lifted the device to her face, the chair leg slipped out. Xander tried to catch it, but he was too slow. The wooden leg clattered on the tiled floor.

Quest's voice boomed. "What was that? Rainbow, Sage. Check it out."

"Run," hissed Xander.

They ran to the stairwell. When they reached the doorway, they turned to look back. The doors to the morgue were open. A red-haired woman with a ragged jean jacket peered out. Behind her stood a stocky man with a bushy beard.

"The kids!" she shouted. "They're back!"

The bearded man yelled, "Get them!"

A half dozen squatters poured into the hallway.

This time it was Priya who yelled, "Run!"

Chapter Nine

Xander ran past Li and Priya and vaulted up the stairs two at a time. Fear had given his legs fresh energy. He nearly grabbed the railing for support before he spotted the barbed wire coiled around it.

He scrambled to the main level and bolted through the doorway. Then he leaned against one of the large filing cabinets and tried to shove it toward the door. It wouldn't budge.

"Give me a hand!" he yelled as Priya and Li burst out of the stairwell.

Priya slammed the door shut behind her while Li pressed her shoulder into the cabinet. It scraped against the tiled floor, screeching like fingernails on a chalkboard. Priya joined in. The filing cabinet lurched along until it was wedged up against the door.

Just in time. Thumps echoed on the blocked door as the squatters slammed against it. The door nudged open a crack.

Xander yelled, "We've got to push more stuff against the door!"

Priya and Li shoved another cabinet toward the door while Xander used his weight to keep the door from opening any wider. They slammed the second cabinet in place, knocking the door shut.

"That won't hold them for long," Priya said.

"It should buy us time to get out," Xander replied.

"What about Omar?" Li cried.

More thumping against the door.

Xander looked from the door to Li and Priya. He couldn't abandon Omar, but there was no way they were going to fight this many people. An idea dawned on him. He pulled the girls away from the door.

"Li, find a hiding spot. Priya and I will lead the squatters away. When you think it's clear, go down and free Omar. When you're safe, text us, and we'll find a way out."

"Okay. I just need a..." She headed to the overturned wooden chair that Xander had pulled apart for weapons. She unscrewed the last of its legs and slapped the makeshift club against her palm. "Ready."

"Find a place to hide," Xander whispered.

She slipped into one of the rooms near the stairwell while Xander and Priya navigated the obstacle course to the other end of the hall.

Priya snapped on her headlamp. "Turn yours on too, Xander, so they can see us."

Xander switched on his light and climbed over the gurney blocking the end of the hallway.

The door finally squealed open, and the first of the squatters burst through. The woman spotted Priya immediately.

"Quest! I see them!" she yelled.

A tall man with long, scraggly hair and a fringed leather jacket emerged from the stairwell. He patted the woman on the shoulder.

"Good work, Rainbow. Now let's get them!"

The rest of the squatters scrambled through the obstacle course, moving like a swarm of angry ants.

"Go!" Priya shouted at Xander.

He sprinted away while she tipped over the gurney. He reached the intersection and glanced back. Priya hurtled toward him with the squatters in hot pursuit.

At the back of the group, Quest yelled, "Don't let them escape!"

The plan was working.

"Li, wait for us!" Xander shouted, pretending his friend was up ahead. "Priya, hurry! We have to catch up to Li!"

Priya ran slow enough to give the squatters a chance to close the gap. Then she joined Xander around the corner.

"This way," Priya said as she took the lead.

"Where does this take us?" Xander asked.

Priya answered, "The cancer ward."

"How do you know your way around this place so well? I'm seriously lost right now."

Footsteps thudded behind them. Xander hoped they had lured all the squatters away. If not, Li was going to have her hands full rescuing their friend.

"Come on, Xander!" Priya shouted. "Down here."

She veered onto another corridor, her headlamp showing the way. Xander raced after her. There was no need to go slow. The squatters could see their lights.

He caught up to Priya at another intersection.

"Did Li text yet?" Priya asked, panting for air.

He pulled his phone out of his pocket and checked the screen. "No."

"How much time does she need?"

Xander peered over his shoulder. "As much time as we can give her."

"Let's go!" Priya shouted as she sprinted to the left.

"Stop!" Quest yelled. "Don't go down that way!"

Xander peeked over his shoulder. The squatters were closing the gap. They held up lanterns and were bathed in an eerie orange glow.

"Dude, we just want to talk to you!" the long-haired man called.

"You'll have to catch us first!" Xander screamed back as he took off. He sprinted toward Priya's light, following it through a series of corridors until he crashed into Priya's back.

"What's wrong?" he asked.

She pointed ahead at the web of yellow tape stretched across the corridor. Just beyond the tape, ceiling tiles dangled above a deep crater in the floor.

"Whoa," Xander said. "Let's try to double back."

He turned around. Too late. The squatters rushed around the corner.

"We have to go through," Priya said. "Follow me."

She tore down the plastic tape and inched along the floor. Xander hugged the wall, his backpack scraping against the slimy surface.

Quest yelled, "Stop! Don't go any farther!"

They ignored him and continued making their way past the hole. The squatters reached the broken web of tape.

"They're almost on us," Xander said. "Move it, move it."

Priya took another step.

Crack!

The floor gave way under her feet. Xander reached for her arm, but she slipped through his grasp and fell downward. She grabbed the edge of the remaining floor and clung to it.

"Help!" she screamed. "I can't hold on."

Another loud *crack* as the floor started to give way.

Xander grabbed her wrists. He tried, but he wasn't strong enough to lift her out. Priya was going to fall in.

Chapter Ten

Xander could feel his grip on Priya slipping. She clawed at the floor, trying to grab anything.

"I can't...hold on...much longer," Xander grunted.

"Don't let go!" she screamed.

"I'm trying not to," he groaned.

She started to slip out of his grasp.

Suddenly another set of hands reached out and grabbed Priya's arms—right before she fell. It was Quest.

He was stretched out on the moldy floor. Behind him, the other squatters had a hold of his legs.

"I've got her," Quest said. "Pull us back."

Xander was stunned. The squatters were helping. They hauled Quest back while he pulled Priya out of the hole. She scrambled to safety at the end of the hallway. Xander inched away from the hole and joined her.

Quest dusted off his jacket and smiled at Priya. "You okay?"

"Why did you save me?" she asked.

"What do you mean? You needed help," Quest said.

Xander shifted closer to his friend. "Thanks."

"No problem," the woman in the ragged jean jacket said. "I'm Rainbow. This is Quest. That's Sage with the beard." She pointed to the others. "Destiny, Marley, Dusk and Ocean."

Xander was stunned that they were being so friendly. "I'm...I'm Xander," he stammered.

"And I'm Priya. And...uh...thanks." She was still a bit shocked by what had just happened.

"No problem, Miss Priya." Quest gave a little bow.

"Good to meet you," Rainbow said. "Now do you want to tell us what you're doing here?"

"We were playing *Spirits and Specters*," said Xander. "It's a role-playing game where we pretend to be ghost hunters looking for evidence of the supernatural."

"Sounds trippy," Quest said. "Find any ghosts?"

Priya shook her head. "It's just an excuse to visit creepy abandoned places."

"Creepy? Not cool, man, not cool," Sage said. "This is our pad, man. Where we crash, you dig?"

"We're sorry," Xander said. "We didn't think anyone was living here."

Rainbow sighed. "We were hoping to keep it that way."

Xander eyed the group. "So what are you going to do with us?"

Quest leaned forward and growled, "You're never getting out of here."

Priya froze. Xander gripped her hand, waiting for the worst.

After what seemed like forever, Quest leaned back and laughed. "The look on your faces, man. Totally priceless."

Rainbow shook her head, a big grin on her face.

Sage clapped his hand on Quest's back. "Good one, man."

Quest motioned to the open hallway. "You cats have to leave now. Just don't tell anyone we're crashing here."

"You know this place isn't safe," Xander said, nodding at the broken web of yellow tape.

Rainbow nodded. "Yes, but we know where the dangerous spots are. Plus, it beats living on the street. Weather's turning. The fuzz are always busting on us."

"The fuzz?" asked Priya. What the heck did that mean? she thought.

"You know, the police," said Sage. "They're always riding us, man, cramping our style."

Xander looked at Priya. He wondered if she was thinking what he was thinking. These people were very odd. And they sounded like they were from another time.

"And if we can't get a bed at the shelter," Rainbow continued, "then we're stuck outside no matter how cold it gets."

"I'm sorry," Xander said. "I didn't realize."

"Not many people do," Quest said. "Out of sight, out of mind."

"What's that mean?" Xander asked.

Rainbow explained. "People like you, well, they deliberately ignore us. Go out of their way to pretend we don't even exist."

Sage added, "Then when they do see us, they think we're going to do something bad."

"Well, you did kidnap our friend," Priya pointed out.

Rainbow glared at Quest and Sage. "I told you that was going too far."

Quest apologized. "We wanted to put a scare in the kid so you all wouldn't come back. I swear we weren't going to hurt him."

"This place is that important to you?" Xander asked.

Sage nodded. "It's our home."

"Here we can just be ourselves," Rainbow explained. "We don't have to be ignored or judged or harassed. Never mind. You wouldn't understand."

Priya grabbed Rainbow's hand. "No, I think I know what you're talking about."

Quest scratched his head of scraggly hair. "You've been on the streets?"

"No, but I know what it's like to get looks from people who see you just one way. It's horrible. You want to yell at people to stop with the pity stares."

Sage frowned. "I hate the look the fuzz give us, man. Like they automatically assume we've stolen something."

A woman with braids and an oversize tie-dyed shirt added, "Or what about those old ladies who'd rather pet a stray cat than give us spare change? They look at us like we're filthy rats."

Xander looked more closely at the group. Their strange outfits made them look like time travelers from the 1960s. He wondered if they had found their clothes from a bin at the back of a thrift store. If they had to root through dumpsters for food. Beg for money outside office buildings. He felt ashamed, realizing he was one of those people who would have prejudged them.

"People don't see you for who you really are," Priya said. "They see you as a thing."

Xander raised an eyebrow. "Wait a minute. Priya, how do you know how they feel?"

She sighed. "Xander, you know how you've been wondering how I knew the hospital so well? A few years ago I spent a lot of time here. I was a patient.

And for the record, they weren't experimenting on anyone. That's just a stupid creepypasta some jerk made up and put on the internet."

"I didn't know you'd been sick," Xander said.

"I had leukemia when I was in third grade. I had to come here for treatments all the time."

"Bummer, man," said Sage.

"Yeah, that's harsh," said Rainbow.

"Why didn't you ever tell me?" Xander asked.

"Because it's a part of my life that I'd rather forget. I lost all my hair from the chemo. Do you know what it's like to be eight years old and totally bald? The kids at school would stare. Some would ask hurtful questions like, 'Are you going to die soon?' or 'Are you still contagious?' Then they'd make fun of me like I was some kind of freak."

"I'm sorry. I didn't know."

"That was the worst. People feeling sorry for me. Grown-ups looked at me with pity, like they only saw my disease. They'd ask how I was feeling, or they'd tell me I was so brave, but they just wanted to get out of talking to me as fast as they could."

Xander stared down at the floor. "I wish you would have told me. I wouldn't have pushed for the hospital location so hard."

"But then you'd have known, and that would have changed the way you treated me," Priya said.

"I wouldn't have treated you differently. You're better now, right?" Xander said.

"See? You're already changing the way you see me." Priya turned to the squatters. "Trust me when I say this. I don't ever want to come back here again."

Rainbow stepped forward and hugged Priya. "I believe you. By the way, I think you would have looked beautiful without hair."

Quest glanced at Xander. "Can you keep our secret, dude?"

"You did save Priya's life. We owe you for that."

"You think your friends will talk?" Sage asked.

Li and Omar! They had forgotten all about them.

"Not when we tell them what you did for us," said Priya.

Xander's pocket buzzed. "My phone," he explained to the others as he pulled out his device.

"Whoa, man. Never seen a phone like that before," Sage said.

Xander checked the screen. There were quite a few messages from Li.

Omar and I are safe.

Where are you two?

Xander! Please answer. We're worried.

The police are on their way.

Chapter Eleven

"We don't have much time before the cops get here," Xander said. "We have to get you out of the hospital."

Quest crossed his arms over his chest. "No way, dude. We're not leaving our home."

Rainbow and the others started to file down the corridor.

"Quest, we have no choice," Rainbow said. "They'll arrest us and lock this place up. We have to split."

Priya had an idea. "I know! Text Li. Tell her to call the police back and say it was a false alarm."

Xander shook his head. "They'll still come. They do it in case a criminal is forcing the victim to say everything is okay."

She raised an eyebrow. "Are you sure?"

"Happened to my dad when he butt-dialed 9-1-1."

Rainbow took action. "We don't have much time then. If it's a busy night, we might have an hour before the fuzz show up. If it's a slow night, less. Gather your stuff, everybody. Just take what we can't replace easily."

The others jogged down the corridor. Quest refused to budge. "This is such a drag, man. I worked so hard to make this place our home. I can't just give it up."

Xander's stomach started to get queasy. He felt really bad for getting these people in trouble.

"They're going to have to live on the streets this winter, and it's all my fault," Xander said to Priya. "All I wanted to do was play *Spirits and Specters* in a new setting."

Priya cracked a smile. "That's it. Good idea, Xander!"

"What? What did I say?"

She shouted after Rainbow, "Hold up! We can fix this so you don't have to leave."

The group turned around and looked at Priya.

Quest said, "They're going to search the hospital. They're going to know we're here."

Priya shook her head. "I know a place where they won't look."

Rainbow beamed. "Really? Well, it's worth a shot."

Sage pulled at his beard. "No way, man. The fuzz aren't going to stop looking until they find us."

"Not if we give them our explanation for why people are here," Priya said.

Xander frowned, confused. "Why else would Li call the cops?"

"The game," she said.

Her words hung in the air for a second before Xander figured out what Priya meant. "Yeah! It just might work."

"I don't get it," Quest said. "How is your game going to help us?"

"Our friend called the police because she saw you here," said Priya. "All we have to do now is make them think this was all a setup for our ghost-hunter game."

Xander pulled the portable speaker out of his backpack. "We'll say that the voices Omar heard were so realistic that his imagination got the better of him."

"But the only way it will work is if we clear all your stuff out of the morgue," Priya said.

"What are we waiting for?" Quest said. "Let's split!"

The group sped through the maze of corridors.

On the way Xander texted Li.

The squatters are ok. We're helping them. Will explain later.

A few seconds later, Li's reply pinged back.

WHAT?

There was no time to explain everything right now. Li was just going to have to trust him.

Tell them you only *heard* people in the basement. You didn't *see* anyone. And text me when the cops show up.

In the morgue, everyone was gathering their gear. They loaded sleeping bags, lanterns and tools into garbage bags. Ratty suitcases that were duct-taped together were stuffed with clothes just as ratty-looking.

Priya grabbed one of the lanterns and set it on the metal examination table screwed into the floor. "Leave this here."

"Why?" Rainbow asked.

"We'll need it for the story we're spinning for the cops."

"Hurry up, people," Quest said. "We have no idea when the fuzz will get here."

Xander shoved cans of food into a green garbage bag and surveyed the morgue. It was going to take at least an hour to clear everything out of here. His phone pinged. He reached into his pocket and pulled it out. The text on the screen was the news he had been dreading.

Cops are pulling up now.

"We're out of time!" he shouted. "They're here! We have to go now."

Priya led the group back to the stairwell. "No one is going to find you in my hiding spot."

"Are you sure?" Rainbow asked.

"Positive," Priya said.

They ran through the corridors, turning corner after corner. Xander, at the rear of the group, half expected a cop to jump out at every turn. Finally they reached a different wing of the hospital. "Where are we?" he asked.

"Sometimes when I didn't want to get another treatment, I hid in different parts of the hospital," said Priya. "It got to the point where my mom wouldn't let me go to the bathroom by myself because she knew I was going to take off."

They jogged to the far end of a corridor. Priya stopped at the door and shoved it open to a stairwell. Barbed wire blocked the staircases.

"We have to go up," she said. "You're going to have to crawl under the wire."

Priya pulled her sleeves over her hands, grabbed a coil of barbed wire and hoisted it high enough for Quest to crawl under. Rainbow followed him. The others passed their things through, then joined their companions.

Xander had to buy them more time. He texted Li.

Stall them.

He waited for an answer. Nothing. Not even the three dots. This was not good.

He followed Destiny as she squeezed under the barbed wire. Priya followed, carefully setting the wire back down.

Thankfully, the barbed wire was only on the first flight of stairs. Now they could move faster. Priya pushed her way ahead of the group and led them to the eighth floor. She opened the door at the top off the stairs and guided everyone through.

Then she led them along the corridor until she found the door marked *Chapel*.

"The police won't look for you here," Priya declared.

"You sure about this?" Quest asked. "I mean, it doesn't look very hidden away."

"Not the chapel. Let's go inside. I'll show you." Priya guided them to a door at the back of the room. It opened to the roof, where there was a patio overlooking the hospital grounds. The red and blue lights of the police car flashed below.

Sage smiled. "Awesome. The fuzz would never think to look for us here."

"And we can see when they take off," Destiny added.

"You just have to watch out for any weak parts of the roof," Priya said. "And there's a fire-escape ladder right there if you have to get down in a hurry."

"Thank you, my lady." Quest bowed to her and then held out his hand to Xander. "Gimme some skin. This is radical."

Xander hesitated, not sure what to do, then slapped Quest's palm.

"You only have to hide here for a bit," Priya said. "When the police are gone, you can go back into your home."

Rainbow hugged Priya. "Thank you. You're good people. I'll catch you on the flip side."

Priya walked over to Xander and pulled him to the door.

"Now comes the hard part," she whispered.

"What are we going to do?" he asked.

"We have to make sure the police won't search for them," Priya said.

Chapter Twelve

With her headlamp lighting the way, Priya navigated their route back to the morgue. Xander followed, panting for breath as he clung to the straps of his backpack.

She skidded to a stop at an intersection. She signaled Xander to duck. Ahead, light spilled from the hallway leading to the obstacle course of furniture.

"We're too late," Priya whispered.

They squeezed themselves flat against the wall and listened.

"Okay, now are you sure this is the hallway?" a female voice asked.

Li's voice answered, "I'm not sure, officer. Everything looks the same."

Priya snapped off her headlamp, lowered herself to all fours and crawled over to peer around the corner. Xander snapped off his light and followed.

Down the hall Li, Omar and two officers stood in front of the chairs blocking the double doors.

"And you say you heard the people down this way?" the officer asked.

Li answered, "Yes, I'm pretty sure that's where they were."

"Tell me again why you two were in the hospital."

"Well, it's kind of a weird story," Omar said. "We heard this place was haunted. And we wanted to check it out. It's part of a game we play."

Another officer laughed. He sounded like a tuba. "I can't believe they're still telling stories about George Wickerman Hospital."

"Do you know what they did?" Omar asked. "They say the doctors experimented on TB patients."

The tuba cop shook his head. "Kid, you heard wrong. Trust me. My uncle used to work here. There were no experiments. There are ghosts, but not from any experiments."

"Really?" Omar asked.

The female officer grunted. "Hawkes, stop pulling the kid's leg. Stay here. I'm going to check out the basement."

"Watch out for the ghosts, Perkins," Hawkes said as his partner moved between the chairs.

Priya turned to Xander. "We have to stop her from going to the morgue or she'll find Quest's camp."

"I have an idea," said Xander, pulling the portable speaker out of his backpack and turning it on. "Find a room to hide in."

Priya crawled across the hall while Xander thumbed through his phone screen until he found the app he needed—Sound FX.

"Psst," Priya hissed.

He glanced up. Priya waved and pointed at the door beside her. Xander gave her a thumbs-up. He peered around the corner and slithered across the floor, hoping the officers wouldn't spot him. When he was halfway across, a voice on the speaker announced, "Your speaker is now connected."

"Hold up, Perkins! You hear that?" Hawkes asked.

Xander shoved the speaker behind him and scrambled toward Priya.

"Hide," he hissed.

She slipped into the room with Xander close on her heels. Footsteps thudded behind them as the door swung closed.

Xander frantically scrolled through the sound-effect options in the app and stabbed at one titled "Ghostly voices."

He waited for a beat as the crack under the door lit up from the officer's high-intensity flashlight. The footsteps thudded closer to the room. Xander slid closer to Priya and grabbed her hand. They were going to be caught any minute now.

"*You belong to us,*" a chorus of ghostly voices echoed from the speaker. "*You belong to us.*"

The flashlight faded from the crack under the door, and the footsteps retreated from the room.

"Over here, Hawkes," Officer Perkins called.

"*You belong to—*" The voices were cut off in mid-chant.

"It's a portable speaker. Kids, this thing belong to either of you?" Perkins asked Li and Omar.

"Sorry. Never saw it before," Omar said.

"Does this sound like the voices you heard?" Perkins asked.

"Maybe?" said Li.

Xander whispered to Priya, "I think it's working.

As long as Li and Omar play along, we might pull this off."

Before she could respond, the door swung open and a figure appeared in the doorway. A bright light flashed in Xander's eyes.

"Show me your hands!" Officer Hawkes ordered, his flashlight aimed at both of them.

Xander immediately obeyed, his phone still in hand. Priya slowly raised her hands too.

"Who are you?" Hawkes asked. "What are you doing here?"

"Sorry," Priya said. "We're with the other two."

"Get up," he growled.

The pair slowly climbed to their feet.

The steel-jawed Hawkes motioned at Xander. "You. With the phone. Explain yourself. Why were you hiding in here?"

"Sorry, we didn't know you were the police."

"Out," he barked.

They stumbled out of the room. Hawkes herded the pair down the hallway. Li and Omar stared helplessly at their friends.

"This yours?" Perkins asked. She held up Xander's portable speaker.

"Yes," Xander mumbled.

Hawkes grunted. "Care to explain yourselves?"

Priya jumped in. "It's complicated. We're in a live role-playing game called *Spirits and Specters*. We pretend to be ghost hunters who explore abandoned places in search of—"

"No, wait, let me guess," Perkins said. "In search of spirits and specters."

"Yes," Priya said. "To spice things up, we try to scare each other."

Xander added, "I was using my speaker to play creepy voices so that Omar and Li would think the ghosts were here. I thought we might be able to scare them out of the hospital, but I didn't think they'd call the police." He shot a glance at Li, hoping she'd take his cue.

She caught on. "You *jerk*," she said. "You could have let us off the hook before I ran off. I thought I was going to have a heart attack."

"Sorry," Xander said. "I just wanted to make a good jump scare."

"Well, congratulations. You pulled it off," Omar said.

Perkins handed the speaker to Xander. "You know you kids aren't supposed to be trespassing on private property."

"We didn't know," Xander said. "We just thought the place was abandoned."

"It's dangerous. Old building like this, you could get trapped, and no one would know you were here."

"I told you we shouldn't have come," Priya said.

The police officers sized up the four teenagers.

"We could haul you in and see if the owner wants to lay charges," Perkins pointed out.

Xander's eyes widened. Priya turned pale. Omar's lips trembled. Li was the only one able to speak. "Please don't. My mom would kill me. *Please*."

Omar joined in. "We won't come back here—we promise."

Perkins let her threat hang in the air, eyeing the panicked kids. She took her time, switching her gaze from one scared face to another. Finally she spoke. "This time I'm going to let you off with a warning. Clear out of here and don't come back."

Omar said, "Yes, officer."

The others nodded and agreed. "Yes. We're not coming back. Ever."

"Okay. Let's get you out of this place," Perkins said.

Hawkes led the way. "Yeah, we don't want those ghosts to get us. Oooo."

"Shut up, Hawkes."

Xander cracked a grin at Priya as they headed down the hall. They had saved Quest and Rainbow's home.

Chapter Thirteen

Perkins climbed into the police car parked outside the hospital, grabbed a clipboard and a pen from the seat and began writing. Hawkes stood with the kids at the side of the car, the red and blue lights striping across his face.

Omar stuffed his hands in his pockets and approached Officer Hawkes. "You said there were ghosts in the hospital. Who are they?"

Hawkes glanced at his partner filling out paperwork, then turned to Omar. "Do you really want to know?"

"Please," Omar said.

"Okay, I'll tell you. But you have to keep it to yourselves." Hawkes stepped away from the car, drawing the kids nearer to him. They gathered around.

"Were there really experiments done here?"

Hawkes shook his head. "No. There were no experiments of any kind. My uncle worked at the Wickerman as an intern in the 1960s. He said this was just a normal hospital until one day when disaster struck."

"What happened?" Li asked.

"There was a fire in the psych ward," Hawkes explained. "The firefighters tried to rescue everyone inside. My uncle said they got most of the patients out, but there was a group of people who were convinced the firemen were government agents. They locked themselves in one of the rooms. They refused to come out, and the fire got to them before the firefighters did. They all died in that room."

"Then what happened?" Omar asked.

"After that night, my uncle said, the ghosts of the dead patients haunted the hallways. They would follow people through the hospital, but you'd only hear footsteps. They also liked to push furniture around. Beds would roll by themselves across a room. Chairs would be stacked on top of each other. Gurneys would flip over on their own. The nightshift nurses were so scared, they asked for an escort whenever they had to walk to their cars. Sometimes the ghosts would whisper strange things in people's ears. My uncle said once he heard a ghost tell him he'd catch him on the flip side."

"Is that story real?" Priya asked. "Or is it just a creepypasta?"

"A creepy *what*?" Hawkes asked.

"Urban legend," Xander explained. "A ghost story."

"Oh," Hawkes said. "Well, I don't know. It's as real as any story about this place is. Believe what you want. I just know that my uncle was relieved when he was finally able to retire."

Perkins poked her head out of the car window. "Okay, you kids head home. This is your one and only warning. Stay away. Understand?"

They all nodded.

"Now get going," she ordered.

The kids hurried down the block, away from the police car and the haunted hospital. Priya kept glancing back at the car, which did not pull away.

"Do you think they're going to search the hospital for Quest and his friends?" Priya asked.

Xander shook his head. "I think they bought our story. They're probably just going to sit there for a while to make sure we don't come back."

"Now do you want to tell us what's going on?" Li asked. "First you tell us to call the police. Then you tell us to stall them. What's the deal?"

Omar agreed. "Yeah, those squatters scared the crap out of me, and you're helping them?"

Xander explained what had happened with Quest's group. He left out the detail of Priya's illness. He thought that was her story to tell, not his.

"So they didn't want anyone to know they were living in the hospital," Xander concluded. "That's why they were trying to scare us away."

"I'd hate to be on the street when the temperature drops below freezing," Omar said. "Still remember when I first moved to Edmonton. I was seven, and I had never seen snow in Egypt. I thought the sky was falling, I was so scared. And it was so cold that first winter, I don't think I wanted to leave the house for a month."

Priya laughed. "That's so cute. I'd love to see the photos of you from back then."

"Mom bought me a winter coat that was *waaaaay* too big. I looked ridiculous in it," Omar said.

Li stopped and patted her body. "Oh no. I left my backpack in the hospital."

"Well, the cops aren't going to let us back in," Priya said. "How important is it, Li?"

"My tablet is in it," Li said. "I can't leave it behind."

"Seriously?" Omar said. "The cops let us off with a warning. I'm not going to take the chance of getting arrested for your tablet. Leave it, Li."

"I can't," she said. "My mom will kill me if she finds out I lost it."

"Maybe we can come back tomorrow and ask Quest and Rainbow to grab it," Xander suggested. "I mean, they're going to come outside at some point, right?"

"Not a bad idea," Priya said. "We keep our word to stay out, and Li gets her tablet back. Sound good?"

Li agreed.

Omar shrugged. "Still think we should just stay away."

The next day the group met outside the hospital. The building looked way less creepy in the daylight. The police were long gone. Xander and Priya walked around the parking lot, searching for signs of Quest and his friends, while Li and Omar remained outside the fence.

Xander cupped his hands and yelled at the roof, "Quest! Rainbow! Sage!"

Either the squatters had gone inside the building, or they were too high up to hear him. Xander and Priya gave up calling and returned to their friends.

"Tough luck, Li," Priya said. "I think your backpack and tablet are long gone."

"We have to get my stuff," Li insisted.

Omar held up his hands. "No way. I'm not about to get arrested."

Xander scanned the block. No one was around. "Okay, you can keep watch. I'm going in."

"Forget it," Omar said. "We promised we'd stay out."

"It won't take long. You stay here. No sense everyone getting in trouble."

Xander jogged to the window entrance, grabbed the edge of the plywood and pried it away from the wall. Suddenly a hand grabbed his shoulder.

"Going somewhere?" a voice whispered.

His breakfast lurched to the back of his throat. Was it the cops?

He slowly turned around. Priya grinned at him. "Gotcha!"

"What are you doing?" he asked.

"I know my way around the hospital. We'll get in and out faster if I come with you. I told Li to text us if she spots trouble."

"What about Omar?"

"He left. He's halfway home by now. He didn't want any part of this."

"You know, I always thought Li was the chicken," Xander said. "But I guess Omar's got her beat."

"She's only scared when it's a game," Priya said. "Omar's petrified when it's for real."

They climbed into the room and headed to what had been home base. Their things were spread across the counter just as they had left them. Priya picked up Li's backpack while Xander cleared out the props on the counter. He noticed the bag of kitty treats.

"You think Rainbow and Quest are okay?" he asked as he picked up the bag.

"Want to check on them? Maybe they can tell us where the real ghosts are," Priya joked.

He laughed. "Okay, just give me one sec."

Xander headed toward a closed door down the hallway and shook the bag. Behind the door, the cat meowed. Xander scattered the treats onto the floor and opened the door. The cat strolled out and started to eat the treats.

"Now we can go," Xander said.

Priya chuckled. "Never took you for a cat lover."

Xander smiled. The two of them then headed up to the chapel. The room was empty. No sign of the squatters or their gear.

"Maybe they're on the roof," Xander said.

Priya opened the door and peered out. "No one's out here either."

"Where did they go?"

"Maybe the police found them," Priya suggested.

Xander let out a sigh. "I thought the cops bought our story. I'd hate for Quest and his friends to lose their home."

"Let's check out the morgue," Priya said. "Maybe they moved back down there."

They dashed down the stairs and made their way toward the basement. However, as Xander approached the corridor leading to the stairwell, he noticed something different. The cabinets, gurneys and chairs that had been stacked up as an obstacle course were gone.

"You think the cops cleared this out?" Xander asked.

"I don't know," Priya said. "I suppose they could have."

They went down the empty corridor and reached the stairwell. Now barbed wire was strung across the staircase.

"No way anyone could have replaced the barbed wire that fast. They'd have to get a crew in to do this," Xander said. "What's going on?"

"Only one way to find out," Priya said.

They lifted the barbed wire, crawled under and went down to the basement. When they reached the morgue, the doors were wide open, and the room was empty. Dust covered the floor, body lockers and examination table as if no one had been in the place for years.

"You sure this is the right room?" Xander asked.

Priya pointed at the sign over the doors. *Morgue.*

The kids searched the other rooms. No sign of Quest or Rainbow or anyone else. They returned to the morgue and stood in the middle of the empty room.

"It's like they were never here," Priya said, her voice echoing off the walls.

"Did it suddenly get cold in here?" Xander asked.

"Maybe we should go. I'm sure Quest and Rainbow's group will be okay."

"Yeah. I guess," Xander said as he turned back to the hall.

"Hey, thanks for not telling Li and Omar about my time here," Priya said.

"I figured some things in the past are meant to stay in the past."

"You mean like the ghosts of the haunted hospital?"

He smiled. "Yeah, right."

"*You belong to us,*" a ghostly voice answered.

Xander spun around, his hair standing on end.

Priya laughed, holding up her phone. She clicked on the screen and replayed the eerie voice. "*You belong to us.*"

"Har, har," Xander said. "Not cool, Priya."

"Made you jump."

He rolled his eyes. "No way. I knew it was you all along."

They strolled out of the room while still arguing about whether or not Xander had been scared. The morgue doors swung closed behind them. Written faintly in red across one of the metal doors was a message:

Catch you on the flip side.

Acknowledgments

Many thanks to Michelle Chan, Wei Wong, Tanya Trafford, Arlene Lipkewich, A. Blair McPherson School, Kathy Oster, Delton Elementary School and all the students who begged me to write a scary story.

Excerpt

Par couldn't join me for my training session on Sunday. His dad had grounded him for breaking the lamp. So I was on my own to go over the drills and routines for my "lesson." I went down to the local rec center.

I had borrowed my dad's sweats. They were about two sizes too big for me. That was a good thing though. No chance of any embarrassing rips with these baggy pants. I practiced the horse stance in front of the mirror, carefully swiveling my feet out.

After a few minutes I noticed Megan in the reflection. She was over at the other end of the gym. She was working some bicep curls. Her sleeveless T-shirt showed off her muscular arms. She must have sensed me watching, because she turned around. I resumed my horse stance, pretending I was focused on my own reflection.

Megan grunted and pumped a few more curls before setting the weights on the floor and wiping off her bench. She walked toward me.

"Nice horse stance," she said.

"What? I mean, oh, yeah. Thanks."

"So the rumors are true. You do know kung fu."

I straightened up. "What are people saying?"

"That you're some kind of martial arts expert. I think I overheard someone say you trained with Jee Ling over the summer. And somebody else said you're related to Jackie Chan."

"Yeah, well, you know what rumors can be like."

"So you're not related to Jackie Chan?"

"Actually, I'm his second cousin."

"What? Really? That's so awesome!"

I laughed. "No, I'm just kidding. The only thing we have in common is that we're both Chinese. That's it."

"Oh. Still, it's cool to meet someone else who is into martial arts."

"So you're into kung fu?"

She punched her fist into her palm and bowed. "Been training since I was nine. My brother was taking kung fu lessons, and Mom only had time to drive us to one activity a week. She gave me a choice. I could do my homework while he was doing his kung fu, or I could join in. Now he's the one sitting on the sidelines doing *his* homework."

"Wow, since you were nine. You must be pretty good. What belt do you have?"

She cocked her head to the side. "You in kung fu or karate? Belts are for karate."

"Oh, right. Yeah, I knew that," I said quickly. "I meant *sash*. I'm so used to people asking me what belt I am that sometimes it's easier to just say *belt*."

"I hear you. I'm blue. You?"

"I'm black and blue," I joked. "Tough drills."

Megan looked at me a little strangely. "So where do you train?"

"Oh, you wouldn't know my studio."

"Is it Gingwu? Wing Chun? I know all the kung fu studios around here."

I inched away from Megan, eyeing the exit. If she pressed much more, she'd figure out that I was lying.

"Actually, I'm in between studios right now," I said. "Anyway, I should probably get back to my workout." That was my lame attempt to change the subject.

"Well, if you want, we could train together."

Megan did a flurry of air punches in front of me, turning her hands into knife blades as she twisted her body and moved toward the mirror.

I nodded. "Not bad. Not bad at all. I'll have to think about it."

"Come on, Jon. I'd like to have someone at my level to do forms with. The only class that I can get to has no one of my age and level. I have to do forms with eight-year-olds."

"Maybe."

"Okay. Well, I'm always up for a training session. You text me, or I'll text you." She unclipped her phone from her armband and swiped a thumb across the screen. "What's your number?"

"Uh...well...I'm not..."

"You between phones too?"

I laughed. "No, no." I gave her my number. I had no intention of training with Megan. But I had to get her off my back.

After she had keyed in my number, Megan glanced up. "You know, everyone is pretty excited that you're going to show off your moves at school next week."

"Yeah, well, I thought it might be a way to get people excited about coming to my sifu's studio."

"I thought you said that you were between studios."

"Right, right. Well, to be honest, it's kind of embarrassing." Oh man, this was hard! "The reason I'm between studios is because mine isn't getting enough students to stay open all the time. My sifu is struggling. I thought this might be a way to get him new students."

"Wow. That's honorable," said Megan. She looked impressed. "My studio," she continued, "is super busy. My sifu complains he barely has time to clean up after all the little kids who come to his classes. I wish we had some older students. Hey, maybe I could visit your studio and train with you there. I know you're probably more skilled than I am, but I can try to keep up."

Time to check my invisible watch. "Oh man. I'm running late. My mom's supposed to pick me up in five minutes. I have to go. See you at school?"

I hustled out of the gym, not daring to look back. Sifu Jon's number three lesson? When you're in the presence of a real kung fu expert, say little and get out as fast as you can.

CHECK OUT MORE GREAT READS IN THE

Orca *currents*

Fishel doesn't like regular "boy" things. He hates sports and would prefer to read or do crafts instead. And everyone but him seems to have a problem with that.

FISH OUT OF WATER

Joanne Levy

orca currents

Jenny is looking forward to her March Break retreat. Until she finds out that the boy who bullies her at school is going too.

Jelly Roll
Mere Joyce
orca currents

Pia has a plan, the perfect plan, but it's looking more and more like today is going to be a complete disaster.

Pia's Plans
Alice Kuipers
orca currents

Marty Chan is an award-winning author of dozens of books for kids, including *Kung Fu Master* in the Orca Currents line and the award-winning Marty Chan Mystery series. He tours schools and libraries across Canada, using storytelling, stage magic and improv to ignite a passion for reading in kids. He lives in Edmonton.

For more information on all the books

in the Orca Currents series, please visit

orcabook.com.